READING CHAMPION

D1493232

Guinea Pigs on the Loose

by Cath Jones and Alex Patrick

W

FRANKLIN WATTS

LONDON•SYDNEY

Chapter 1

Becks was very excited. She was looking after the school guinea pigs for the weekend.

"Hello, Fluffy," Becks whispered. "Hello, Ginger. I will take good care of you, I promise."

Two little pink noses poked out of the hay.

"Eek!" squeaked the guinea pigs.

Becks had a lot to do. First, she made sure the hutch was in the shade. She didn't want the guinea pigs to get too hot.

Next, she topped up their water bottle.

Then, she added fresh hay to their bed.

"Is that alright?" she asked quietly.

"Eek!" squeaked Fluffy.

Becks wondered if the guinea pigs had to stay in their hutch. At school, they had a run to play in. Maybe she could build them a run, too. Becks fetched some things from the garden shed and set to work.

When the run was ready, Becks slowly opened

the hutch door. At first, nothing happened.

Then, the two guinea pigs jumped out

and began to munch the grass.

Becks ran into the house to fetch Mum.

She wanted her to see the run. But when they

came back into the garden, the run was empty!

Chapter 2

"Don't worry," said Mum. "We'll find them."

Mum and Becks searched everywhere.

But there was no sign of Fluffy or Ginger.

"Where are they?" said Becks.

"Fluffy! Ginger!" she called.

Then she heard a quiet rustling sound
and some squeaking. It was coming from
Mum's vegetable plot.

Quietly, Becks crept up the garden path.

Yes, there was Ginger. He was hiding behind

a large orange pumpkin in Mum's vegetable plot.

And there was Fluffy, munching the lettuces.

Becks started to tiptoe towards them ...

but too late!

Becks and Mum chased after them,

but the guinea pigs were too fast.

"Oh no," Becks cried. "Please come back."

Fluffy and Ginger did not come back.

Then Mum said, "Listen!"

Becks heard squeaking. It was coming from

behind the shed.

Slowly, quietly, Becks crept

closer and closer to the side of the shed.

There was no sign of the guinea pigs.

But then Becks spotted a hole in the fence.

Chapter 3

The guinea pigs had gone into next door's garden. Becks was a little bit scared of the man who lived there. His name was Mr Konetch. He always got cross when her football landed in his flowerbeds.

He would not be happy about having two guinea pigs in his tidy garden. She had to get Fluffy and Ginger back quickly.

Becks and Mum peered over the fence.

Becks was surprised. Mr Konetch's garden

did not look very tidy at all.

"Mr Konetch is away at the moment," said Mum.

"His grass is much longer than usual. I think

he is coming back today or tomorrow."

"Quick, maybe we can catch Fluffy and Ginger before he gets back!" Becks said. "Oh, dear. I can't see them anywhere."

"Look!" said Becks, pointing. "There they are!"

There, near the fence, were Fluffy and Ginger.

They had already munched a little pathway

through the long grass.

Chapter 4

Becks had a plan. She fetched an old fishing rod from the shed.

"Fluffy, Ginger," she called and dangled a carrot over the fence.

"Eek!" squeaked the guinea pigs.

Their noses twitched.

Becks pulled the carrot along the ground.

The guinea pigs followed. They were almost

at the hole in the fence when Becks heard

the sound of a car. She heard a door slam.

Mr Konetch came striding up his garden path.
He looked around happily. He stopped and sniffed
a flower. Then he stopped and stared at the fence.
"Guinea pigs!" he cried.
"Eek!" squeaked the guinea pigs,
munching happily.

"Oh dear," Becks said quietly.

Mr Konetch bent down and scratched the top of Fluffy's head. He tickled Ginger's ears.

"Hello, Mr Konetch," Becks said nervously.

Mr Konetch smiled at Becks.

"Um, I can explain ..." said Becks.

Mr Konetch laughed and picked up

the two guinea pigs. "Thank you!" he said.

He handed Fluffy and Ginger carefully over
the fence to Becks and winked.

"What a clever idea," he said, "using your guinea
pigs to mow my grass while I was on holiday!"

Things to think about

1. Why do you think Becks decides to make the guinea pigs a run?
2. How else might Becks get the guinea pigs back?
3. What would have happened if Mr Konetch had not come back when he did?
4. What do you think Becks might do differently when she lets the guinea pigs out again?
5. Will Becks and Mr Konetch become friends now?

Write it yourself

One of the themes of this story is pet care. Can you write a story with a similar theme?

Plan your story before you begin to write it.
Start off with a story map:

- a beginning to introduce the characters and where your story is set (the setting);
- a problem which the main characters will need to fix;
- an ending where the problems are resolved.

Get writing! Try to use interesting noun phrases, such as "a quiet rustling sound", to describe your story world and excite your reader.

Notes for parents and carers

Independent reading

This series is designed to provide an opportunity for your child to read independently, for pleasure and enjoyment. These notes are written for you to help your child make the most of this book.

About the book

Becks has the responsibility of looking after the school guinea pigs for the weekend. She looks after them well, but those guinea pigs are just too tempted by next door's garden!

Before reading

Ask your child why they have selected this book. Look at the title and blurb together. What do they think it will be about? Do they think they will like it?

During reading

Encourage your child to read independently. If they get stuck on a word, remind them that they can sound it out in syllable chunks. They can also read on in the sentence and think about what would make sense.

After reading

Support comprehension and help your child think about the messages in the book that go beyond the story, using the questions on the page opposite. Give your child a chance to respond to the story, asking:

- Did you enjoy the story and why?
- Who was your favourite character?
- What was your favourite part?
- What did you expect to happen at the end?

Notes for parents and carers

Independent reading

This series is designed to provide an opportunity for your child to read independently, for pleasure and enjoyment. These notes are written for you to help your child make the most of this book.

About the book

Becks has the responsibility of looking after the school guinea pigs for the weekend. She looks after them well, but those guinea pigs are just too tempted by next door's garden!

Before reading

Ask your child why they have selected this book. Look at the title and blurb together. What do they think it will be about? Do they think they will like it?

During reading

Encourage your child to read independently. If they get stuck on a word, remind them that they can sound it out in syllable chunks. They can also read on in the sentence and think about what would make sense.

After reading

Support comprehension and help your child think about the messages in the book that go beyond the story, using the questions on the page opposite. Give your child a chance to respond to the story, asking:

- Did you enjoy the story and why?
- Who was your favourite character?
- What was your favourite part?
- What did you expect to happen at the end?

Franklin Watts
First published in Great Britain in 2020
by The Watts Publishing Group

Copyright © The Watts Publishing Group 2020
All rights reserved.

Series Editors: Jackie Hamley and Melanie Palmer
Series Advisors: Dr Sue Bodman and Glen Franklin
Series Designers: Cathryn Gilbert and Peter Scoulding

A CIP catalogue record for this book is
available from the British Library.

ISBN 978 1 4451 7234 7 (hbk)
ISBN 978 1 4451 7239 2 (pbk)
ISBN 978 1 4451 7244 6 (library ebook)
ISBN 978 1 4451 7880 6 (ebook)

Printed in China

Franklin Watts
An imprint of
Hachette Children's Group
Part of The Watts Publishing Group
Carmelite House
50 Victoria Embankment
London EC4Y 0DZ

An Hachette UK Company
www.hachette.co.uk

www.reading-champion.co.uk

FSC
www.fsc.org
MIX
Paper from
responsible sources
FSC® C104740